Red Dragon

A Bestiary of Modern Britain

A Note from Elsewhen Press

When we published Simon Kewin's Witchfinder series book *The Seven Succubi* (the second story of Her Majesty's Office of the Witchfinder General, protecting the public from the unnatural since 1645), it referenced Dr Miriam Seacastle's modest book *Red Dragon*, which was privately published by the author herself in 1999 in an illustrated, limited edition. We were keen to obtain a copy but discovered that there were no extant copies available. In his own book, Simon had mentioned that the OWG in Cardiff had a copy, so we sought permission to examine it. After much obfuscation and bureaucracy, we managed to contact the librarian directly. With a little persistence they were persuaded to allow us to peruse their copy in a secure facility. We were able to make a photographic record, which is what we have used as the basis for this facsimile edition.

We subsequently obtained permission to reproduce *Red Dragon* from Dr Seacastle, who expressed delight that her book would once more see the light of day, but conveyed her concern that all copies would again be seized by the OWG. We assured her that we are firmly of the opinion that this book is an invaluable collector's item, and we will robustly resist any attempt to suppress its republication.

We also obtained the approval of the illustrator to use the original illustrations in this facsimile.

You can find more about Simon Kewin's books in the back papers of this volume.

Red Dragon

A Bestiary of Modern Britain

Dr Miriam Seacastle

2022 Facsimile edition

Elsewhen Press

Red Dragon

Originally privately published by Dr Miriam Seacastle, 1999

This facsimile edition published in Great Britain
by Elsewhen Press, 2022
An imprint of Alnpete Limited

Elsewhen Press, PO Box 757, Dartford, Kent DA2 7TQ
www.elsewhen.press
British Library Cataloguing in Publication Data.
A catalogue record for this book is available from the British Library.

ISBN 978-1-915304-05-6 Print edition
ISBN 978-1-915304-15-5 eBook edition

Designed and formatted by Elsewhen Press

Contents

WARNING

THIS BOOK IS THE PROPERTY OF THE LIBRARY OF THE OFFICE OF THE WITCHFINDER GENERAL.

IF FOUND, IT SHOULD EITHER BE RETURNED UNREAD OR IMMEDIATELY DESTROYED. NOTHING IN IT SHOULD BE REPRODUCED IN ANY WAY.

BY ORDER OF
THE WITCHFINDER GENERAL
WHITEHALL, LONDON, SW1A 0ET

Foreword

As a girl, I was fascinated by the beasts and creatures that filled my story books and my imagination – but that the learned volumes of science insisted did not, in fact, exist. In truth, it was worse than that: the books didn't even attempt to argue that dragons, the fae etc. were imaginary – instead they simply ignored the more cryptic ranks of fauna completely, not even attempting to investigate the countless sightings, clues and traces that have come to light over the years.

Of course, there can be no doubt that many such creatures *are* purely imaginary. As a species, we delight in inventing and imagining no end of horrors and wonders, filling the shadows with details that our eyes and our scientific instruments cannot discern. This fact does not mean that everything (currently) unknown to science must necessarily be illusory. To take but one example, I have known a great many sceptical and dismissive scientists who see no inconsistency in then worshipping a divinity and perhaps, even, believing in angels and demons or whatever it may be. I make no arguments either way about the wisdom of such beliefs; I simply point out that the attempts of science to measure and catalogue are limited by the technologies and even the ideas that we currently possess. We are studying nature through cracked and warped lenses, and we may even be using the wrong sorts of instruments completely.

Once, the idea of microscopic creatures – creatures we cannot see but that can move from person to person causing disease – would have been dismissed as madness. Many scientists did indeed ridicule the notion of tiny "animalcules" as fanciful. Today, of course, we know that the microscopic legions are vast and hugely varied. The point is this: what we know now does not define everything that we *can* know. We are stumbling about the cave with our guttering torches, slowly exploring, but the cavern is vast and there are passageways and levels in it that we haven't yet even glimpsed. At best, we may catch their distant whispers echoing towards us...

This slim volume is an attempt to catalogue a selection of the creatures and entities for which there is clear (or at least highly suggestive) evidence within these isles – although, in many cases, they are creatures inhabiting much greater domains than this small archipelago. They are visitors to our shores. I believe everything in it is real, or at least that each entry hints at some organism whose actual nature is yet-more indistinct, hard to detect or remarkable. What this book is *not* is comprehensive. By definition, I assert, it would be impossible to catalogue every cryptozoological entity, as the creatures are obscure, esoteric, elusive – or they dwell in dimensions of reality that we do not, yet, have a full understanding of. As such, it would certainly be possible to write subsequent volumes. I very much hope that I or others do precisely that.

Meanwhile, stumbling about in our cave, we have to start somewhere. I trust this volume goes some small way towards expanding the sphere of light that is human knowledge.

Dr Miriam Seacastle, Suffolk, 1999

Aethernal

Our familiar, everyday world is connected to every other world and plane of existence by a limitless containing void that we call *the aether*. Every planet and galaxy in every universe exists (if *exists* is the correct term) as a point within this vast metaspace. Some cryptozoologists have suggested that the aether is conceptual, encompassing all possible, theoretical or imagined worlds too – although this is unknown, and the similarities to the *multiverse* proposed by some theoretical physicists is certainly intriguing.

Entering the aether is difficult – although not impossible, especially at certain points on the Earth's surface where the walls are thinner (the distance is less?) between the planes. It is, however, dangerous to leave our domain as it is easy to become disorientated and disconnected in such an immense space. It is not known how many lost souls float through the aether, unable to find their way home, unable to enter any physical realm that they might encounter. The number might be uncountable.

One other danger of the aether is known about, too:

the *aethernal*. These are creatures who naturally inhabit the void. Describing them is arguably pointless, given that scale is meaningless in the aether, but they appear to be shifting in form, cloud-like. Some writers have claimed that aethernals are little more than seething hazes of hunger; entities craving light, energy, complexity. They devour any that they find and grow (again, if *grow* is a meaningful term) as a result. Are there aethernals who have managed to consume entire worlds? Entire universes? It is possible. Such entities would be formidable, indeed.

Several writers have proposed that the incursion of such aethernals through the tears in our reality might account for many sightings and phenomena that we perceive. Ghosts, for example (see below), might simply be the brief appearance of an aethernal into our plane of reality – or perhaps the long-term presence of a small aethernal that has managed to slip through the cracks.

It is also possible that there are many, many species of these creatures, and that their forms and natures are infinitely more varied even than the multitude of life forms we see on our planet. Are some intelligent? It is very possible. One can only hope that such a being, sentient or on the sort of titanic scale that could devour whole worlds, never drifts by our reality in the aether…

Banshee

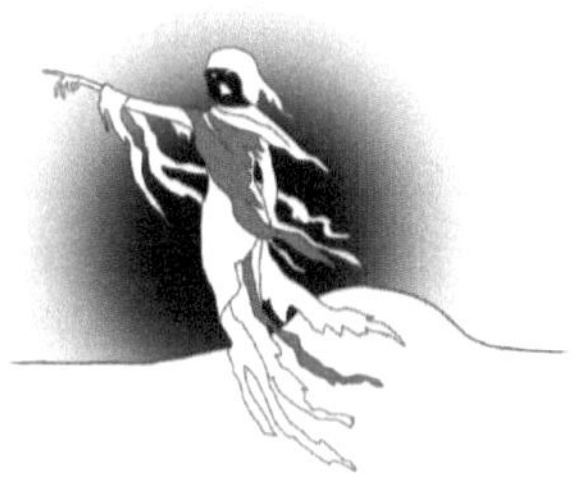

The original banshee (*bean sí* in modern Irish, from *ben síde* in Old Irish, meaning "woman of the fairy mound") lived in the Irish countryside, although similar entities have also been identified in other parts of the British Isles where the Celtic past retains a toehold: particularly Scotland, Wales and the Isle of Man. The creature is often to be found in close proximity to a tumulus or earthwork (hence the Irish name), although they can also reside in close proximity to rivers or lakes.

The banshee is a spirit, whose keening heralds the death of a family member of the individual hearing the cries. The mournful wail – always heard in the depths of the night – is thus a dreaded and terrible sound: the hearer knows that someone close is going to depart the world but has no idea whom. It may very well be *them*. Typically, three cries are heard, on three separate days. On the third day, the death will happen.

Some well-established families or clans are said to have their own, dedicated banshees, and it is also claimed that more than one banshee will sometimes be heard keening in unison, to foretell the demise of some important or notable individual.

No male banshees have ever been recorded – either because they do not exist or because they are particularly elusive. It is possibly a mistake to attempt to impose simple, binary concepts of gender onto a magical creature. Note, also, that variants and entities distantly related to the traditional banshee have been reported – for example, in Wales, there is the *cyhyraeth*: a skeletal, wraith-like figure whose appearance is also said to portend death.

The banshee is not a happy soul: she is often described as having red eyes from her continual weeping and lamentation. She almost always has long, red hair and a ghastly complexion. She might appear to be either a young or an older woman, although whether this is because she can alter her appearance or because she simply grows old as humans do is unknown.

The cry of the banshee can sometimes be heard by those who are far from home, but for many years, it was assumed that the entity was confined to rural areas, becoming rarer and rarer as populations migrated into cities during the industrial revolution. In recent decades, however, it has been noted by experts that the *urban* banshee is becoming more common, as the spirits take up new homes among the towers and streets of our towns. Their cries are often mistaken for the wail of emergency vehicles rushing to some catastrophe, but a careful analysis has revealed that the plangent calls are sometimes to be heard echoing down city streets when *no* emergency vehicles are in the area. One cryptozoologist has noted how precisely this new form of banshee call mimics the rising and falling cadence of an ambulance or a police car, noting that the behaviour makes complete sense: "the sounds produced by such vehicles are often the harbingers of death in the modern world; it is perhaps not surprising that the uprooted banshee would learn to copy them." (Martin Trebuchet in *Life in the Shadows*, 2019).

So, if you find yourself in the city at the dead of night and hear a rising and falling wail coming at you from some unidentified direction, beware: it could just be an ambulance or police car, but it *might* also be the keening of an urban banshee foretelling either your own death, or the death of someone close to you…

Black Dog (Dire Hound)

Black dogs and dire hounds are to be found in stories and reports throughout the British Isles – notable examples including *Black Shuck* (Norfolk, Suffolk, Lincolnshire), *Padfoot* (Yorkshire) and *Moddey Dhoo* (Isle of Man) – but there are many others. It is not known if these are all the same creature, or simply members of the same species.

The creatures are generally reported as large, black beasts, often with glowing red eyes. They are quite frequently spectral in form and are able to change their shape, pass through solid walls and so forth. They can be dangerous and malicious creatures. Several accounts report less ghostly versions of the dogs attacking people in the dead of night, ripping out their throats and baying with blood-curdling howls.

Like the banshee, black dogs are often beasts of portent – to see one is to know that some calamity is about to fall. This brings with it an inevitable sense of despair in those they pursue. If a powerful black dog is pursuing you, there is no escape from it: the beasts are as relentless as they are brutal.

It is perhaps because of this fact that the black dog has become a synonym for depression in the modern world – as if, deep down, folk memories of the beasts survive in all of us.

Bookwyrm

These entities have been known by many names over the years: archaeon, biblid, page walker, ideolon. The most common name ascribed to them, however, is *bookwyrm*. A bookwyrm has no true physical existence: it is a creature that inhabits the realm of ideas and thoughts. In that sense, it is a purely conceptual entity – although the creature does, on occasion, protrude into the physical realm, for example as an image in some ancient tome. For reasons that are unknown, they have a preference for manifesting as colourful, stylized dragons, often wrapped around passages of text. It is possible that this is simply where the entities were first noted, by the mediaeval monks who spent their lives working on illuminated manuscripts such as the *Book of Kells*, in an age when there were few other concentrations of written thought to intrigue the entities.

Some cryptozoologists believe that bookwyrms predate humanity, and that they may even predate the presence of a physical realm in the universe – i.e. that they were alive when reality existed only on a purely conceptual level. Certainly, however, the entities have thrived alongside advanced, sentient lifeforms such as humanity. Bookwyrms crave ideas, knowledge, insight, learning. The written word therefore attracts them enormously, and anywhere where there is a high concentration of words is likely to be home to one or more bookwyrms. Ancient libraries, especially, are their domain. They move from volume to volume, absorbing and learning as they go. It is thought that bookwyrms know every written language and store within their minds an appreciable proportion of all the knowledge that has ever existed.

More recently, there have been one or two reports of bookwyrms jumping the gap from ink and paper books to electronic "libraries" such as the internet. This should come as no great surprise: to the bookwyrm, a library of paper books and the millions and millions of pages on the world wide web are more or less the same thing: knowledge encoded for convenient retrieval. Sustenance, if you like, for the endlessly voracious bookwyrm.

Bridge Troll

Bridge trolls were a persistent danger to travellers in early mediaeval Britain, and many accounts exist of the creatures lurking near to and beneath river crossings (fords as well as bridges) intending to waylay and harass innocent travellers. The earliest accounts suggest that the trolls in question were attacking people in order to consume their flesh, although this may be apocryphal, a deliberate denigration of the troll. Certainly, later accounts describe them using menace and threat to extract goods, food and money from their victims, and it is possible that this was their motivation all along.

Wasteland trolls such as these are now extremely rare in Britain, and they may even be extinct in these islands. It is hard to be sure as so few remnants are ever found: troll skeletons, as is well known, are made of stone rather than bone, and they either crumble to dust or are mistaken for natural rocks, boulders and pebbles when discovered.

The reason for the creature's extinction is a familiar one: habitat loss. The growth of human populations and the spread of what we call *civilisation* may have wiped out a species that is, or was, one of Britain's oldest intelligent natives. This process was certainly accelerated by the efforts of His (now *Her*) Majesty's Office of the Witchfinder General from the 17th century onwards as roads in Britain were improved and the government sought to extract funds from travellers for itself (in order to pay for road improvement with its *turnpike* roads). Several commentators have pointed out, wryly, that this process involved *troll bridges* being replaced by *toll bridges*.

It is possible that small populations of wasteland trolls cling on in wild, upland regions of Britain. It would certainly be welcome to think so. The Office of the Witchfinder General is stretched thinly these days, and creatures such as trolls are seen as less of a priority. It seems likely that many magical species have been able to make something of a comeback as a result – something that is surely to be welcomed.

Cambion

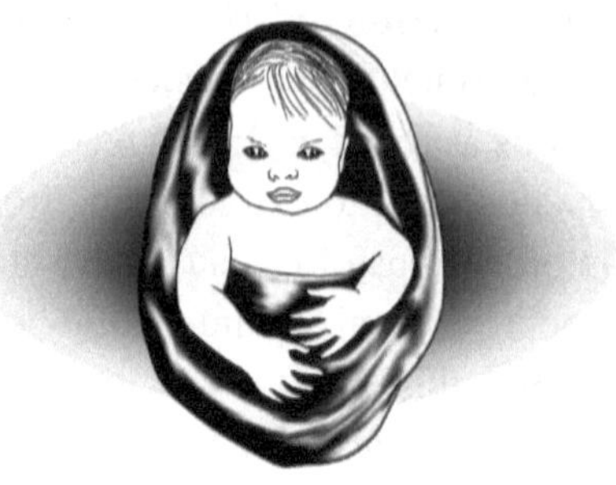

A demonic changeling resulting from an act of procreation taking place between two humans, but involving the intercession of a succubus and an incubus. See the entry on the *Succubus*, below.

Crow King

There are many species of corvid to be found in Britain – as there are in most regions of the world. Crows, rooks, jackdaws, choughs and the mighty raven – these and other birds make up the *corvidae* family according to biological classification. Many corvids are gregarious and highly intelligent – even to the point of using tools.

The Crow King, meanwhile, does not appear in any official ornithological reference. In some sense, it may be considered the god of the corvids, or perhaps their embodiment, their spirit. Sightings of the Crow King are rare, but it has been described by several observers over the centuries as a huge black bird, far larger than any other corvid. It is usually seen in flight, at which times hundreds of crows, rooks, ravens and so on flock after it, mobbing it in adoration, attempting to keep up with it. They never can: the Crow King flies extremely quickly when it wishes to.

Its call is said to be strident and yet oddly musical.

A number of cryptozoologists categorize the Crow King as a harbinger, a creature like a banshee (see above) that appears only when some terrible calamity is about to befall. Others, however, report seeing the bird without suffering any such disaster. Writing in the mid-Victorian period, for example, the amateur naturalist Carena Shuffleforth described watching the bird on several occasions in the Yorkshire Dales, noting its "huge size and beautiful, glossy plumage, the colour of ink, yet shining in the light". Despite making these observations as a young woman, it is known that Shuffleforth went on to live well into her nineties.

A few individuals have claimed that the crow king is a shapeshifter, capable of taking on the form of a person if it so desires. Why it would do so, the reason for it walking amongst us, remains unknown.

Demons and other Summonings

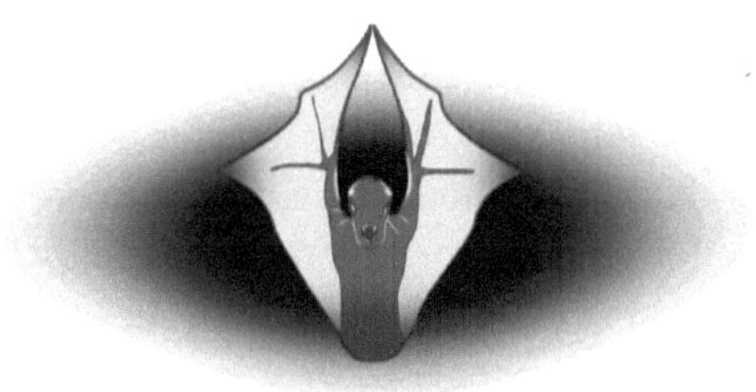

The range of entities from other dimensions and planes of reality is truly vast. Reference works such as Oakblack's *Diabolical Peerage* talk about the "aristocracy of Hell", as if there is a single hierarchy of demons and devils. This is very likely to be an oversimplification. It may even be that there are an unlimited number of domains from which entities can be summoned, just as it may be that some entities come from the aether itself (see the aethernal, above).

There are many reports of such creatures being brought through the veils into our world – sometimes out of curiosity, very often out of malevolence and a desire to do harm. The impulse for self-aggrandizement no doubt also plays its role: many summoners have sought to manifest beings to do their bidding, although anecdotal evidence suggests this rarely goes to plan. The entities summoned may either fail to properly materialise, or else they may manifest *too* readily, overwhelming the supposed defences (spell circles and the like) put in place to contain them.

Some demons (the term is a useful label to cover a wide range of summoned entities and presences) do appear to be more common, whether because the magics required to bring them forth are easier, or because they are simply more widely known. The *pestilential presence*, for example – a hideous, shambling creature whose very touch is death – seems to be a fairly common summoned demon. Again, classification and categorization are difficult without a proper scientific study. It is possible that terms like pestilential presence are used to refer to a large number of unrelated demons.

Doppelganger

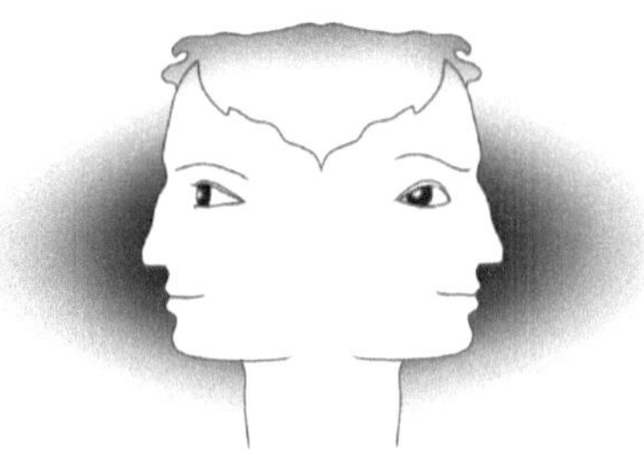

An entity that impersonates a person, mimicking their appearance and nature with uncanny accuracy. Some experts consider these entities to be demonic, while others categorize them as some manner of ghost or spirit with the power to take on a copied physical form.

Doppelgangers are frequently malicious in nature, taking delight in causing harm or upset to their victims. While this can lead to all manner of embarrassing or awkward social situations, there are also several known cases of doppelgangers committing serious crimes – up to and including murder – in order to incriminate the person they are copying. This malice has led some to believe that doppelgangers are actually a nation or type of the fae (see below).

The cryptobiologist Dr Amjit Singh asserts that doppelgangers are capable of copying their victims with extreme accuracy, down to molecular level. As such, even a DNA analysis would be incapable of differentiating between the original person and the impersonating doppelganger. This fact has led to more than one unfortunate individual being convicted of crimes they did not commit. It has also, no doubt, meant that many victims have been diagnosed as delusional when their fervent claims of innocence are "disproved" by science.

Dragon

This volume is called *Red Dragon* because of the familiarity of this particular form of the beast – but it is by no means the only one. The creatures have been reported in a wide variety of colours and sizes. Most have four legs and two wings (two-legged dragons are, more correctly, called wyverns – see below), although some dragons have no wings at all, and simply "swim" through the air as if it were water.

Dragons are often considered to be mythical, and while they are vanishingly rare, it would be wrong to mistake their aloofness and disdain for humanity with inexistence. They are essentially creatures of the sky: unrestricted, uncontrolled, soaring the vaults of air on their great wings and landing only when some urge such as hunger impels them. For them, "sky" is a wide concept; they can fly effortlessly between the atmospheres of any and all worlds, moving (as we would see it) between the realms as if there were no walls in the aether keeping the different domains apart. Perhaps there are not, and it is our perceptions that are wrong. For dragonkind there is only one "sky" in all of creation, and it is a domain of which they are the masters. This is somewhat analogous to the Horned Man, the figure who is a spirit of the woodlands (see below). To him, there is only one forest, and all the forests we perceive are simply a part of it. So, with the dragon: the creatures can fly to whatever regions of the sky they wish to visit, and the exact nature of the particular land rolling away beneath them, the identity of the beings walking around down there, is unimportant.

That all said, dragons were once much more familiar to human eyes and ears. Whether they are rarer now because we have presumed ownership of "our" skies, filling them with machinery and noise, or whether the creatures have simply chosen (for reasons we cannot begin to fathom) to fly elsewhere is unknown.

Dragons in stories and myths often like to hoard vast piles of gold and jewellery – either because they are avaricious, or because they are imbecilic enough to simply like shiny things. In reality, dragons have never been reported slumbering atop mountains of coin. The briefest consideration of such stories will clearly demonstrate how ridiculous they are – they are often set in times when there was little material wealth, making the existence of such vast stores of treasure highly unlikely.

Face in the Mist

This entity is, by definition, indistinct, as it is the denizen of any widespread patch of cloud – be it fog, smog, smoke, water vapour or steam. Some cryptobiologists, particularly Dr Amjit Singh, believe that these beings are, in fact, aethernals (see main entry, above) that briefly find a way to access our realm from the void. Other writers believe these creatures are natives to our world, and that there are a great number of them drifting through the atmosphere, unknown and undetectable until some cloud of particles or vapour gives them a medium in which to manifest. Yet others have cast doubt on the entire claim, asserting that the sighting of forms in clouds is simply a matter of *pareidolia* – that is, our innate tendency to invent faces in everyday objects.

Recent investigations have discredited the pareidolia claim, as it is known that multiple, unrelated individuals report glimpsing the same features in larger patches of mist, cloud or smoke. It is likely that one result of the industrial revolution – with all its clouds of smoke and steam – was a rapid increase in the numbers of these indistinct entities. Malevolent – and extremely large – faces have been reported numerous times in the plumes of vapour escaping from factories and power plants in recent years, although these are inevitably dismissed as "imagination" or "chance".

Widespread pollution has been a fertile breeding ground for them: it is known, for example, that the Great Smog of London in 1952 saw many of these hazy entities – labelled *smokewraiths* or *fogwraiths* – drifting through the streets of the UK capital. Thousands of people died, officially because of the pollution, but the presence of these malevolent, drifting forms also took its toll. It is known that The Office of the Witchfinder General – these days charged with tackling all supernatural threats to the British realm – was central in pressing for the introduction of clean air legislation following the great smog, in order to give these indistinct entities less of a fertile breeding ground.

One other possibility is that *faces in the mist* are the ghosts of the dead, either lingering in a particular locale, or summoned to it by a malign spell worker. They may also be aethernals (see above) manifesting in our world. It is also possible that all these explanations are correct at different times: the entity is, by its very nature, foggy and indistinct.

Fae

Many names have been ascribed to the beautiful, dreadful and capricious denizens of fairy: the Little Folk, Themselves, the Tylwyth Teg, the Fair Folk and many others.

In fact, it is wrong to think of the fae as a single people, just as it is wrong to think of humans in such terms. There are many domains, kingdoms and powers in Fairy. Many of the denizens of those realms are indifferent to humans – or as indifferent as humans might be to ants. Some of the fae, on the other hand, delight in the mischief they can cause people, while yet others are (as we would see it) actively malicious and deeply cruel.

Some cryptozoologists believe that the fae are the animating spirit behind the Wild Hunt (see below).

Reaching the lands of Fairy, or opening the ways so that the fae can reach us, has long been an area of research and experimentation among antiquarians and magical practitioners. One common belief is that there are certain areas (such as mounds in Ireland) which are both in our world and in Fairy. The fae live there, and if you can find your way inside (or are unfortunate enough to be dragged inside), you may never return.

For others, reaching those other lands is a complex and cryptic process. Writing in the late nineteenth century, the antiquarian A. G. Smiles described how he managed to map out a series of intersections "between the woodlands of South Wales, Somerset and parts of Gloucestershire and Herefordshire with the shadow woods of Western Fairy Land". Smiles' methods involved walking certain green lanes, pacing out a complex sequence of "traversals to be undertaken while the moon is waxing to the appropriate degree and the required stars are in the sky". By virtue of this odd, mystical dance, he claimed, he was able to step across the worlds and explore the lands of Fairy.

Unfortunately, Smiles did not record the precise details of his methods. It is known that he disappeared in 1881 and was never heard from again.

Forbidden Alphabets

The name given to certain sets of runes that, when correctly drawn and combined in the required ways – literally spelling – allow powerful magic effects to be enacted. These typically involve the summoning of demonic entities into our realm from across the aether, although it is likely that such runic magic can be used for many purposes, for example creating curses or controlling the minds of victims.

Samuel Bedfellowes, the Victorian investigator and dabbler in the arcane, asserts that "there may be an infinite number of these runes" – i.e. that they exist in some theoretical realm waiting to be discovered. They have their effect, furthermore, "because they resonate with the fundamental forms and laws of Creation". There is no proof on either point.

It is also the case that the runes of the forbidden alphabets can be dangerous and destructive in and of themselves: they can cause physical harm to those they touch, for example by burning, freezing or inflicting agony. This has led some writers to assert that the runes are not merely letters at all, but some form of living entity, capable of attacking those they come into contact with. It is certainly true that the sigils can, in the right circumstances, exhibit many of the characteristics of life. Cases have been described of the runes moving, reproducing and devouring that which they come into contact with – all indicators of a (barely-understood) life form.

Gargoyle

The Reverend R D Pates, the amateur naturalist and scholar writing in the late 19th and early 20th centuries, often found himself with little to do in between writing his sermons. He devoted much of his life to writing his magnum opus, *Investigations into the Transmundane*, in which he catalogued at an almost obsessive length the supernatural creatures he observed in the three English counties of Herefordshire, Gloucestershire and Worcestershire, the area in which he lived.

To modern cryptozoologists, perhaps his most important contribution was his detailed analysis of the gargoyles he observed clustering around the walls of the older churches in his area. These he sketched and catalogued in the greatest detail – so much so that he was the first to observe the creatures' movement: their occasional night-time forays and their slow migrations from building to building.

Pates postulated that the entities we call gargoyles are, in fact, two completely separate entities who have, as he put it, exhibited the sort of symbiotic convergence that Mr Darwin has described, to the point that it is now almost impossible to differentiate between the two different forms of the entity. The first subspecies is a creature something like a small troll, its body stone and its features often (to our eyes) grotesque. These are the original creatures, perhaps once inhabiting mountain crags but who learned that the buildings of humans offer a safe and secure place to slumber.

The second subspecies, meanwhile, is more akin to a possessed statue (see below) – humans, it is thought, seeing the naturally occurring gargoyles, and thinking them simply carvings made by other masons, attempted to reproduce the figures, exaggerating their ugliness, drawing on scraps of knowledge about demons and other such entities, to create the hideous figures still to be seen on old buildings. As with possessed statuary, these gargoyles then acquired or absorbed whatever disembodied souls were passing by (perhaps one reason the entities prefer to flock to churches, with their convenient graveyards) to achieve life.

Pates, somewhat coyly, suggested that the native gargoyles found these carved newcomers *so appealing and comely, that an intermingling inevitably proceeded*. This may well be true. Most modern cryptozoologists accept the dual origins of the gargoyle – and also that, today, there is essentially only a single, hybrid species.

Ghost and Ghast

erms like *ghost*, *ghast* and *wraith* cover a wide variety of incorporeal spirits. Some are the souls of the dead who linger in the physical realm out of confusion, love or anger at some perceived injustice (see, for example, the Malevolent Spirit, below). Others are entities that have never had physical form – e.g. those that dwell in the aether (see aethernal, above) – but that manage to seep through the cracks between the worlds to trouble ours.

Faces in the mist (see above) may, sometimes, be simply the manifestation of some manner of ghost.

There are many, many reports of hauntings to be found in the literature. The majority of these, no doubt, are fallacious: the result of suggestible individuals reacting to odd or suggestive situations. Undeniably, however, there are many real and provable examples of what we might term *hauntings*. To pick just one notable instance, there is the story of Emily Doward, a girl who lived in the East End of London in the 1950s. Emily wrote diary accounts of being visited by a ghostly presence of a girl about her age "wearing tatters of rags and looking very pale and thin." This ghost girl was also called Emily. Unusually, however, Emily Doward's accounts included a great amount of concrete detail about the life and death of the older girl: where she lived, who her relatives were and how she died (of typhus, as we would now call it). There was also the fact that she treasured "a silver bracelet carved with my name, given me by mama".

These details were not written down in any public record anywhere; there was no way for Emily Doward to know them. Two years after the hauntings began, and at Emily's insistence, pits were dug in the back yard of her house, revealing the deeply-buried bones of a young girl. Archaeological analysis dated the bones to the middle of the seventeenth century. Around the wrist of the skeleton was a tarnished silvery bracelet with the word *Emily* just visible.

How the story turned out, and what became of either Emily, is unknown. It is believed that the Office of the Witchfinder General intervened to remove the story from the public eye.

Giant

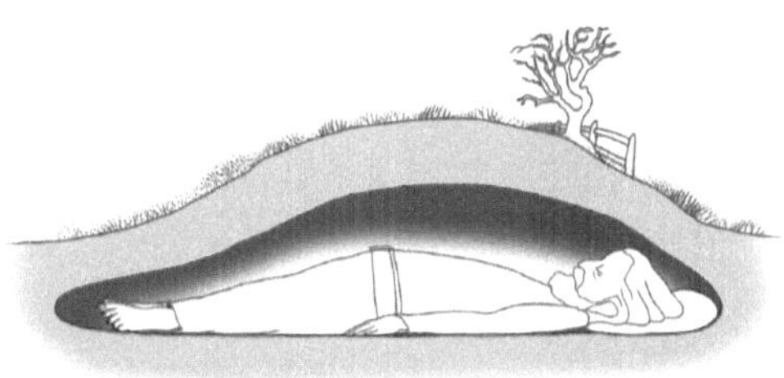

"There are giants in the earth", wrote Agneish Faygold in the seventeenth century, "and it is best that they are left to their long slumbers, for fear of the harm they may inflict on the good and free folk who dwell above the ground."

Faygold was referring to the well-documented cases of giants – figures in human form but two or three times the height of a normal person – who sleep in deep caverns and hollows beneath British soil. It is probably futile to speculate why they are there: as with mound worms (see below) and dragons (see above), it is likely that these entities have been there for a long time, very possibly predating human civilisation. Some writers believe that all of these entities were once much more active, and that either the modern world is not to their liking, or that strong spells were worked in antiquity by unknown spellweavers to keep the creatures magically insensible.

Whatever the truth, it is still possible for these beings to be disturbed, and when this happens, they can be exceedingly troublesome. As is the case with mound worms, the Office of the Witchfinder General has seeded stories about these sites being ancient burial mounds and Neolithic long barrows in order to discourage people from digging into them.

Horned Man

Also called, simply, the Green Man or Herne the Hunter, the Horned Man is a tall, powerful male figure with deer antlers growing from his head. In some accounts, he is able to transform at will into a deer, allowing him to run with incredible speed. Indeed, it is possible that he can become any manner of woodland creature – possibly including the trees themselves. The Horned Man is a sort of guardian spirit or *expression* of woodland; a semi-divine creature that guards and protects the trees and the creatures that live amongst them.

As with dragons flying in the sky (see above), the Horned Man (according to many cryptozoologists there is only one) walks *all* woodland. To him there is only one forest in all of creation: a single, vast sward that happens to be scattered across multiple worlds and planes. These distances mean nothing to the Horned Man: he can step between the worlds (as we would see it), in order to move from one part of "the wood" to another. Indeed, there only needs to be a single, solitary tree for the Horned Man to be a presence.

Insect Swarm

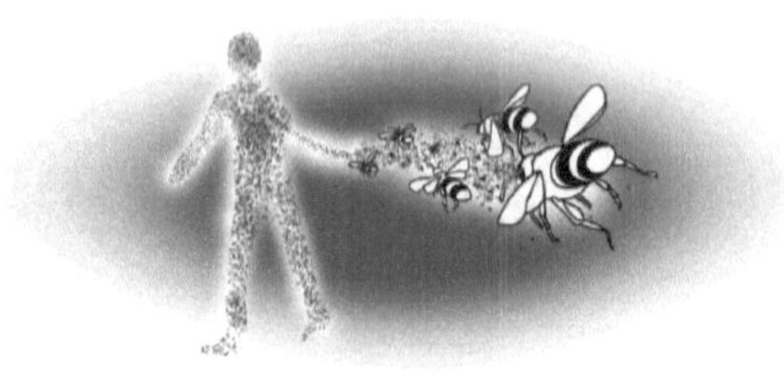

Swarms of insects acting as if they are a single individual have been reported by a number of annalists and observers. These are sometimes loose agglomerations: for instance, a swarm of butterflies that appears to act with a single mind, flocking to overwhelm some object or even person. Writing between the wars, for instance, Henry Lamplighter described in alarming clarity his experience of nearly being suffocated by a swarm of many thousands of Painted Lady butterflies on the South Downs. "My mouth was full of their rustling, clattering flight, he wrote, so many of them that there was no longer any room for air."

Bees, wasps and moths acting in concert have also been reported. It is more common, however, for ground-dwelling insects to mass together and act in this way. There are several reports to be found in the literature of swarms of ants coming together in a single, seething mass. A report from Manchester describes one such swarm forming the rough, shifting outline of a biped – a person – that then attempts to talk, although no words have ever been understood.

These swarms can extend beyond the insect family. The amateur cryptobiologist Elemina Parkend described being pursued by a shifting mass of spiders, worms and "myriad other denizens of the woodland leaf litter" through the Forest of Dean one midsummer's evening. "It took on the loose form of a person," she wrote, "but divided and reformed at will in order to pass among branches or around trees, while the sound it made was of hissing and rustling as it pursued me most rapidly."

Some cryptozoologists believe that these animated masses of tiny life are related to the Face in the Mist (see above), in that both entities involve some spirit using what matter is available to them to acquire temporary corporeal form. The truth is unknown.

Dr Miriam Seacastle

Jenny Haniver

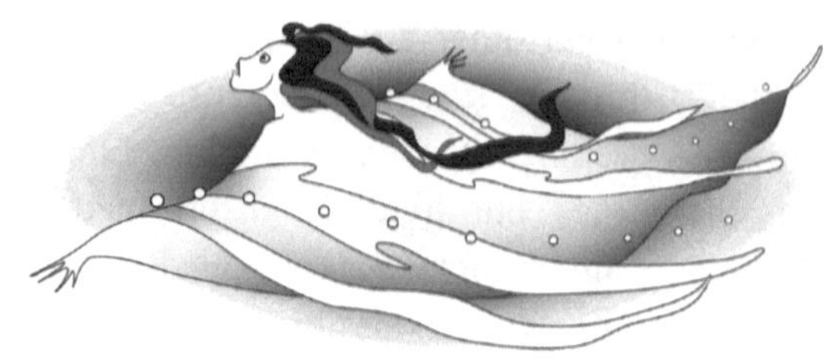

A demonic spirit that dwells in deep waters and cold oceans. Their bodies sometimes wash up on the shore, or else the entities are glimpsed alive by sailors – an event which is considered, like the keening sound of a banshee (see above), to foretell someone's death. It is noticeable how many cryptozoological entities are considered to be harbingers of doom.

Simply looking at a Jenny Haniver is, according to some accounts, fatal – akin to the way that looking at a basilisk (i.e. a cockatrice) can kill the observer. This fact perhaps explains why so few sightings of the creatures have been recorded.

Sailors have been known to fashion their own Jenny Haniver figures, perhaps from the carcass of a skate or a ray, in an attempt to assuage, exorcise or alarm the real entities. Some of these facsimiles are certainly impressive, approaching the true appearance of the creature, and the existence of these reproductions has obviously allowed the truth to be dismissed as fanciful nonsense by the Office of the Witchfinder General.

Kitchen Witch and Corn Dolly

British folklore has many figures such as the kitchen witch and corn dolly – small human-like effigies constructed from twigs, straw, leaves, cobwebs or other naturally occurring resources. These figures are typically good luck charms, created to watch over a house and deter evil spirits, or else they are made to attempt to ensure the harvest is abundant.

Others have a more malign purpose, constructed to act as a focus for inflicting harm on an individual, in a manner reminiscent of the voodoo doll seen elsewhere in the world – although, again, this can also be a way of providing protection against a person or an entity considered to be dangerous or evil. When constructed to target a particular individual in this way, the dolls typically have "something of" the target – a lock of hair or a drop of blood – woven into the fabric of their forms.

Dr Miriam Seacastle

Lurker Beneath

The Lurker Beneath is believed to be a truly ancient lifeform that has crawled through the deep caverns and fissures of the Earth for aeons uncounted. It is unknown if this is an individual of great age or a whole race of creatures. It is even possible that reports of multiple different chthonic creatures have been combined to form this supposedly single entity.

It is thought that the mines and tunnels dug by humans in recent centuries have given the creature a new home – one reason that there tend to be more sightings in areas where deep mines were sunk, e.g. South Wales and Yorkshire. There are numerous reports of it winding its way through such abandoned workings, but also more populated passages – e.g. underground train tunnels in the dead of night. Like banshees and gargoyles, the Lurker has seemingly found a new home in the cities built by humans. More than one deep station in the London underground network has been sealed off by the authorities because of sightings of the Lurker. It is, very occasionally, glimpsed from the surface, e.g. through the grille of some access hatch, but such sightings are always fleeting and indistinct.

Details of the Lurker Beneath are scarce: it appears to be huge, wormlike, almost indestructible, but also mortally afraid of the light. From all accounts, its body is rather fluid as it can squeeze into small ducts and pipes to reach new tunnels, but it also appears to be powerful and strong, capable of chewing through bare rock to escape if threatened.

It is not known if the creature is intelligent, nor what its motivations are for coming near the surface to explore the world of humanity. Very occasionally, it will come into direct conflict with humans, at which time it reveals itself to be vicious and deadly, capable of ripping its victims to pieces. It is unknown whether it attacks for food, or only when threatened.

Malevolent Spirit

Malevolent spirits are often considered to be a species of ghost (see above), but they are distinctive enough to be afforded their own entry in this bestiary.

These entities are incorporeal, but they frequently attach themselves to certain *focus objects* in the physical world in order to manifest. These objects are rarely random: they are usually some totem or memento left over from a person's life that then becomes the lightning conductor for their anguish or fury. Malevolent spirits are the source of many stories of ghosts and revenants troubling people with their "unfinished business", returning to our world to exact their revenge. They can be extremely dangerous to the living. While weaker entities might simply cause alarm or disquiet, the more powerful ones, those seething with their fury, can cause emotional pain, physical harm or even death upon anyone coming into contact with them.

As such, they should be treated with extreme caution. While it is possible for these sprits to be placated (exorcised by the satisfaction of whatever resentment burns within them), the process of so doing is frequently fraught with danger.

Dr Miriam Seacastle

Mound Worm

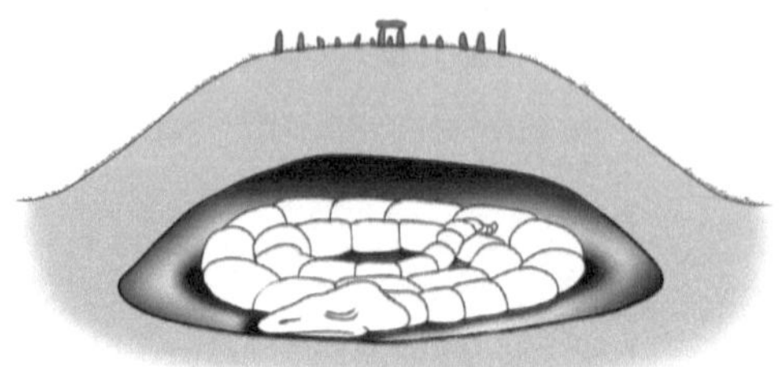

he giant worms that live under the ground have been likened by some cryptozoologists to the *Lurker Beneath* (see above), and by others to dragons. The latter connection is unconvincing; it is only made, possibly, because dragons are sometimes referred to as worms or wyrms. Mound worms are legless, wingless creatures that neither walk not fly.

Mound worms are surprisingly common in the British Isles, although most people will be unaware of them owing to their preference for slumbering away the centuries if left unmolested, as with giants (see above). There are many smallish, round hills to be found dotted around the Britain countryside, (Silbury is one such, but there are numerous others), and a great many of these will have a vast mound worm, perhaps hundreds of yards long, coiled up asleep within.

This fact has been well-known to amateur investigators for many years, but the truth has been kept quiet by the intervention of the Office of the Witchfinder General, who are responsible for the stories about the hills being ancient burial mounds and important archaeological sites and the like, in order to provide a pretext to prevent people digging into them. By these means, the truth is kept quiet and the worms are allowed to continue their long slumbers.

Mound worms do occasionally awaken to venture forth into the world. The reasons for them doing so remain unclear. They appear to largely ignore humans, but there are reports of them casually crushing people who are unfortunate enough to get in their way. As with giants, it is possible that strong magic was employed in antiquity to keep these creatures safely asleep in their lairs – although whether these incantations need to be constantly renewed by some party is unknown.

Possessed Statue

ossessed objects are a truly ancient form of magical entity, certainly predating the time of humans on the planet. Since the earliest days, it was known that all manner of objects could become controlled by some animist entity – perhaps a disembodied spirit life-form, perhaps the soul of one of the departed. Rocks, trees, rivers, swords, thunderclouds – any and all of them can become the home of a controlling spirit. Very often, the object's behaviour is affected: a particularly malicious spirit possessing a thundercloud will give rise to a particularly vicious storm. A calm and gentle river under the influence of a malevolent entity can turn suddenly treacherous, pulling the innocent swimmer into an inescapable whirlpool.

In the past few centuries, possessed statues have become one of the more common manifestations of this type of magical entity. It is, perhaps, easy to understand why: statues are large, discrete, immobile objects set up in places – towns and cities – where many spirits will be gathered. The angry and resentful dead that swirl around in any large human habitation will naturally gravitate towards them. The fact that many statues are metallic may or may not be significant – it is unknown if certain materials are more susceptible to possession than others. Some researchers have speculated that the increased use of metals, particularly iron, since the industrial revolution, is responsible for the increase in possession activity. Perhaps metal attracts the spirits like an antenna receiving a signal, or perhaps a disembodied life-force can, like electricity, more easily flow through metal. It is noted that *all* of our taller city buildings have steel frames – a fact that makes them a magnet for possession and which, perhaps, explains much.

It is likely that at least some gargoyles (see above) are possessed stone carvings.

A particularly fascinating feature noted by experts is the existence of so-called *sculptural determinism*, by which possessing spirits take on some of the characteristics of the statues they possess. It has been noted, for example, that statues of military figures tend to be more combative and brutal when animated than other figures. Similarly, for example, a statue of a large creature such as a lion will *behave* like a lion when animated. It is, in truth, unknown what is cause and what is effect here: does the statue of a military figure affect the behaviour of its possessing spirit, or do such effigies naturally attract warlike spirits?

As so often in an age when the magical and the fantastical are sidelined, more research is needed.

Seething Blob

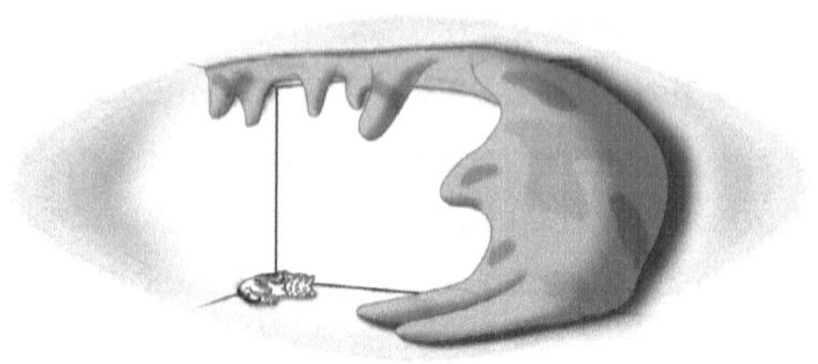

A protoplasmic entity like a mass of jelly, the seething blob survives by engulfing and absorbing its prey – which can be anything organic, dead or alive. Seething blobs are incapable of moving rapidly, but they are relentlessly determined in pursuit of their quarry, meaning that anyone cornered by one will probably not survive the encounter. Seething blobs can crawl up walls and along ceilings as well as across floors. Their malleable bodies also mean that they can squeeze through tiny gaps – under doors, down pipes – before reforming themselves with no apparent ill effects. They can also survive long periods without sustenance. When they eat, they grow larger, and when they do not, they stay the same size or even shrink.

Some cryptozoologists assert that the Seething Blob and the Lurker Beneath (see above) are one and the same entity: a fundamentally formless creature shifting its shape as it needs.

It is not known if seething blobs are intelligent. They do, however, come in many different colours, some of them very handsome indeed.

Succubus

A succubus is an overtly sexual demonic entity in roughly human female form that traditionally attempts to mate with a male victim and by doing so inflict exhaustion, harm, severe mental distress – or even death. While she may appear to be classically beautiful at first glance, certain supernatural bodily features are often present that betray the true nature of the succubus: for example, a curled-up serpentine tail, sharpened teeth or raptor claws.

The male counterpart of the demon is termed an *incubus*. Cryptozoological accounts stretching back for many centuries detail the ways in which succubi and incubi supposedly cooperate to achieve their malign ends. The process is oddly complicated: the succubus acquires the semen of her victim and then passes it onto an incubus, who then uses it to impregnate an unwitting human female with a demonic offspring. By doing so, a *cambion* is formed: a demonic changeling. However, it is never completely clear why this complicated process has to be involved, or quite how it could work – or indeed, why any resulting offspring would be *altered*, since it appears that non-demonic human gamete cells have been involved throughout. No doubt the answer is to do with dark magic.

Descriptions of succubi tend to be lurid, almost pornographic in their detail, and in reading them it is hard to escape the notion that we are learning more about the writer than the supernatural entity. There is a clear misogynistic aspect to these traditional (very often Victorian) accounts: a fear of the female and of female sexuality, and possibly an homoerotic impulse as well. In more recent times, writers such as Cardwell and Beredin, while finding good evidence for the existence of succubi and incubi, have thrown the traditional *modus operandi* described into doubt. Cardwell in particular questions the strictly binary nature of the succubus/incubus distinction – as well as the strongly heteronormative assumptions behind their supposed behaviours. He goes on to speculate that succubi and incubi are, in fact, aspects of the same entity, capable of adapting its form to suit the proclivities of an intended victim. Certainly, this more gender-fluid account of the demon does away with all the complicated semen-exchange activity described so luridly throughout much of the literature.

The precise nature of the *cambion* that results from these unions, meanwhile, is unclear – although it has been reported by several observers that the children exhibit unnatural powers and can be highly dangerous, especially under the influence of the malevolent.

Many accounts exist of the emotional and physical harm inflicted upon those who are attacked by the succubus. It is easy to understand why: while physical exhaustion doubtlessly accounts for some of the damage, the wrecking effect upon intimate human relationships and upon the victim's peace of mind or even sanity must be considerable. Guilt can be a powerful and insidious enemy. It is a sad fact that, unchecked, such liaisons can lead inexorably to the victim's demise.

Unicorn

nicorns are large equids with a single, elegant spike protruding from their foreheads. This horn is seen in both female and male unicorns and is always helical in shape, twisting around to a sharp point. It is known that some horns twist clockwise (*sunwise* in the terminology) and some anticlockwise (*widdershins*). The reason for this is unknown; it may or may not be significant.

Apart from their horns, unicorns are easily-mistaken for large grey or white horses. This situation, and the unfortunate fact that their horns are venerated by some alchemists and wizards for their magical properties, mean that Britain's unicorn population has long-been endangered. As a result, the creatures have been hidden in plain sight by the simple practice of capturing them and removing their horns. The effort is oddly similar to the removal of rhinoceros's horns in order to protect that species from poachers. Unicorns without horns appear to be horses to most observers. It is highly likely that you have seen unicorns but were unaware of what you were witnessing.

Unicorns are, however, both intelligent and elusive

beings. In order to capture them – and to encourage them to appear like "normal" horses once their horns have been removed – strong sorcery has to be employed. Many practitioners consider this to be cruel, but others have argued that it is an acceptable practice if it allows Britain's unicorn populations to survive.

It is not known how many individuals there are in the wild, although the number is probably dwindling. There are also reports of *entire* unicorns – those with their horns intact – being observed in distant corners of the British Isles, e.g. the deep woods of the New Forest. Some cryptozoologists suggest that the presence of these untamed unicorns indicates the presence of the Horned Man (see above). Reliable photographic evidence, however, remains scant.

Vampire

It is interesting that popular myth has many of the true details of vampires more-or-less correct, even if it is wide of the mark in certain significant respects.

Vampires are not, technically, "undead" (as they do not die in order to become what they are) – although they are certainly not human either. They *do* demonstrate impressive physical strengths and have quite incredible abilities, but they aren't immortal. In popular myth, they live for ever until beheaded or pierced through the heart with a stake. In actuality, while they may live for many centuries, they do slowly succumb to the effects of ageing and decay. It is arguable that they don't ever really (completely) die: they simply fall into the sort of torpid slumber from which there is no awakening (unless in the most extreme circumstances). Examine the family crypts of several branches of the British aristocracy and you will find the final resting places of many great old vampires from bygone eras. These beings are no longer active, but nor are they quite dead – a possible source of the *undead* notion.

While they *are* active and "young", vampires are among the most fearsome foe for those who devote their lives to attempting to eliminate the monstrous and the "unnatural". They are extremely hard to harm as they regenerate rapidly if injured. They are not afraid of holy symbols (of any faith) and they are not troubled by garlic. They are also tolerant of sunlight: again, it is possible that all those crypts with their ancient slumbering vampires have given rise to the false impression that the creatures crave the darkness. They cannot transform themselves into bats or wolves, but they can project their minds into these creatures (and just about any others), in order to take control of them. They do wield strong magic of their own, typically to coerce those around them into behaving against their character.

Vampirism *is* a trait that is passed on from individual to individual, although this is not a simple matter of being bitten in the manner often seen in films and books. The decision to bestow the gift (or the taint, depending on your perspective), is never taken lightly: typically, it is given to the chosen successor of a family line, or to some other revered clan member. This demonstrates a fundamental point: in the British Isles, vampirism is strongly associated with the aristocracy. It is used in the same way that wealth, privilege and deference are used, namely to maintain the social distance between the aristocracy and the *commoners*. Vampires are almost exclusively wealthy and titled, from families able to trace their roots back over many, many centuries.

Inevitably, a cabal of vampires has often been found at the heart of the British establishment, quietly exerting its influence over monarchs and, in more recent centuries, governments. It is thought that more than one prime minister has been a member of this group. It is known that the House of Lords – the UK's upper legislative chamber, made up partially of unelected hereditary peers – has always contained at least two or three vampires. This cabal even has a name: the Order of the British Vampire. The name originally arose as a joke among a small circle of aristocratically-connected vampires at Eton school in the 19th century, as a tongue-in-cheek reference to the *Order of the British Empire* (the *OBE*, an honour bestowed upon those achieving great things). Today, the Order is very serious indeed – and, doubtlessly, very powerful.

Wild Hunt

It is debatable whether the wild hunt as a beast or living entity even exists. While some cryptozoologists have proposed that it is, indeed, real – some sort of formless, ghostly presence that influences or controls the corporeal – others have dismissed this notion as lacking proof. For these writers, the wild hunt is a cultural practice, a tradition, and nothing more.

Yet other writers assert that the malicious influence of some nation of the fae (see above) is responsible for the manifestion of the hunt. They cite *the delight in sport and slaughter* that some denizens of Fairy exhibit.

Whatever the truth of it, I'm including the wild hunt in this bestiary for the sake of completeness. The term describes a group of hunters – frequently spectral or demonic in nature – pursuing their quarry on horseback. The wild hunt is frequently accompanied by spectral hounds that may well be some relative of the black dog or dire hound (see above). Wild hunts are often associated with particular figures. e.g. local deities or figures from folklore. The essential nature of the hunts remains the same: a wild, headlong pursuit of some poor victim, frequently at night and sometimes through the sky. More recent incarnations of urban wild hunts have also been reported – packs of red-eyed wraiths on demonic motorbikes pursuing their unfortunate prey through the night time streets. The Hunt is an unstoppable force; once it is in full flight, its quarry is doomed.

Some cryptozoologists assert that the wild hunt is yet another harbinger, and that its appearance foretells some dire calamity beyond the inevitable death of the pursued victim. For the record, I doubt this: the accounts I am familiar with suggest that the wild hunt is undertaken for no reason other than blood-crazed, madcap fun.

Wyvern

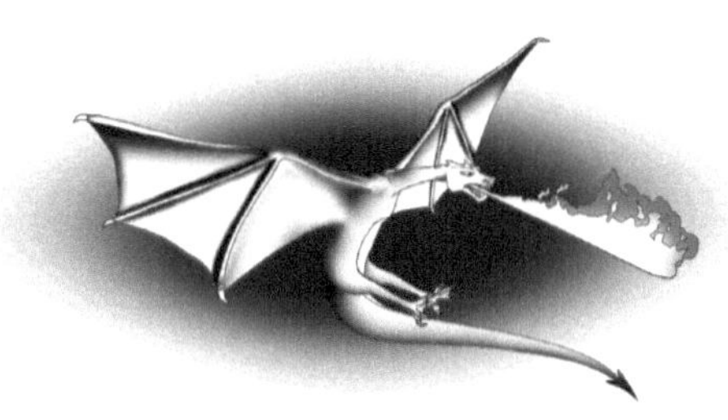

Wyverns are similar in many ways to dragons (see above), and some cryptozoologists consider that they are variants of the same species – or at least that the two can intermingle. Wyverns are large, winged, tailed, fire-breathing creatures, typically with two legs as opposed to the dragon's four.

As with dragons, wyverns are much rarer these days than they once were. Also, as with dragons, wyverns consider there is only one sky, a vast expanse of air that spans all worlds and that wyverns can fly through as they wish. This is why, as we would see it, the creatures are rarely seen these days. They have chosen to spend most of their time elsewhere – as they would see it, in another part of the sky.

About the Author

Dr Miriam Seacastle is Visiting Professor of Cryptozoology at the University of All Albion. She has long been fascinated by the creatures and beasts who lurk in the shadows of our perception and that step only warily out into the bright light of reality. She is the author of several works on the subject, including *Nightmares and Other Beasts*, *The Hidden Kingdom* and *Fantastical Creatures: an investigation into Mythozoology and Cryptozoology*. She focuses mainly on the shadow fauna of the British Isles, but also spent several years researching the entities to be found in the Middle East and North Africa.

In her spare time, she gardens, compiles crosswords and collects antique teapots. She lives with several cats and a human, none of which, so far as she is aware, are supernatural in any way.

Acknowledgements

My eternal gratitude to Dorothy Aphrodite Coldwater for her invaluable insight and support during the assembly of this little book. Many of the entries would not have been possible without access to the tomes and scrolls in her keeping – and, indeed, to the impressive store of information she carries in her mind.

My thanks also to the author Simon Kewin for his invaluable advice and input on the layout and editing of this book.